# THE SAND HORSE

Atheneum
Macmillan Publishing Company
866 Third Avenue, New York, NY 10022
Collier Macmillan Canada, Inc.
First American Edition 1989    Printed in Italy

10 9 8 7 6 5 4 3 2 1

Library of Congress Cataloging-in-Publication Data
Turnbull, Ann.
  The sand horse.
  Summary: At the seashore, a horse sculpted
from sand yearns to ride with the white horses
galloping on top of the waves.
  [1. Sand sculpture—Fiction.  2. Horses—
Fiction.  2. Horses—Fiction.  3. Seashore—
Fiction]  I. Foreman, Michael, 1938–    ill.
II. Title. PZ7.T8493San  1989  [E]  89–9
ISBN 0–689–31581–3

# The Sand Horse

Story by Ann Turnbull
Pictures by Michael Foreman

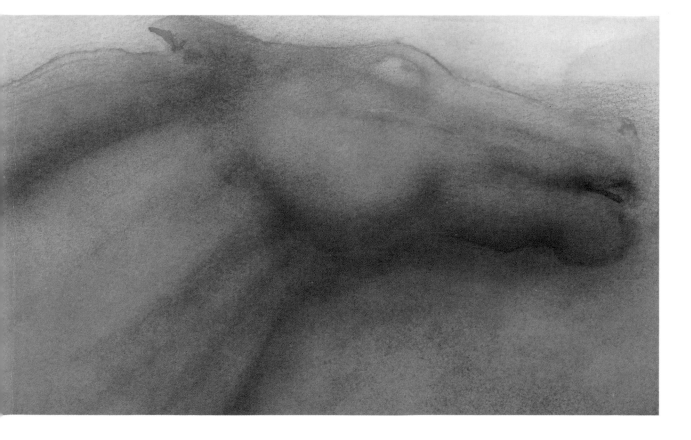

Atheneum          1989          New York

Once there was an artist who lived in St. Ives. He lived with his wife and baby in a house by the sea. Sometimes the artist worked in his studio, but on fine days in summer he went to the beach and made

animals in the sand. He could make dogs and cats and seals and
dolphins, but mostly he made horses, because horses, he said, were
the most beautiful animal of all.

One morning the artist woke to a brisk blue day with a choppy
sea and white crests on the waves.
"Look! White horses!" said his wife.
When the sea is rough and the waves have white tops, people
sometimes call them white horses.

The artist saw them: far out in the bay, plunging and galloping, tossing spray from their manes.
"Today I shall make a horse," he said.

He went to the beach. He marked out his area, put his hat down
on the sand, and started work.

First he fetched water from the sea. He splashed some onto the dry sand. He patted and molded the sand.

The horse began to appear: muscles and hooves, raised head and rippling mane.

The beach filled up with people. They stopped and admired the sand horse. They threw money, and the coins chinked in the artist's hat.

The horse grew. He was a galloping horse, galloping forever on his side.

All day the artist worked on his horse, shaping the muscles of his legs and neck, twisting each curl of his mane.

He worked until the sun set and the beach grew cold. Families began leaving. They folded their deck chairs and shook sand from their clothes.

The artist scooped up the coins in his hat and went home.

The sand horse woke up.
He was alive, but he could not move. He opened his one eye, but
all he saw was clouds. He listened with his one ear. He heard
sea gulls. He heard the boom and hiss of the sea. And, faintly, in the
crash of waves, he heard neighing.

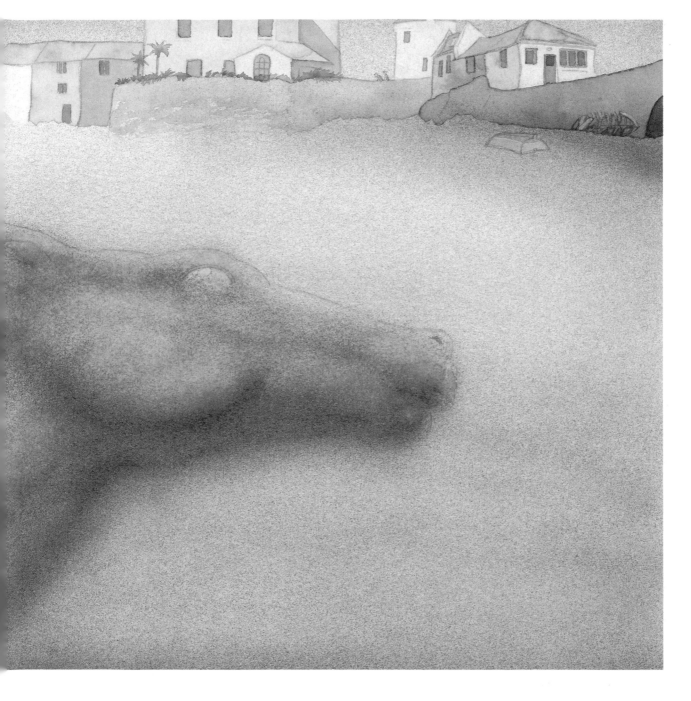

A sea gull landed on his back and walked about, jabbing the air with his sharp beak.

"Sea gull," said the sand horse, "what's that neighing I hear?"

"That's the white horses," said the sea gull, "out in the bay."

"What are they doing?"
"They are prancing and frisking and flicking their tails."
"Where are they going?"
"Everywhere!" said the sea gull. "Newlyn, Polperro, Mevagissey,
Marazion —"

"I want to go with them!" cried the sand horse.
"You!" The sea gull wheeled up in the air, laughing, and all his friends joined in. He swooped down again and said, "You! You are only a sand horse. You can't go with them."

The sand horse tried to move. He was a galloping horse, but he was fixed in the sand. He could not go with them.
The sky darkened. The sea gulls flew away. The boom of the sea was louder.

Much closer now, the sand horse heard the white horses neighing.
"Come with us!" they called.
The sea crashed on the shore, flinging spray over the sand horse.

"Come with us!"
The sea crashed again, and the sand horse was soaked with spray.
"Come with us!" called the white horses. "To Sennen, Land's
End, and the Longships Light!"
A wave broke and flooded the sand horse, drenching his head
and mane.

"I'm coming!" he called. "Wait for me!"
Another wave broke, and the sea ran foaming all around the
outline of the sand horse, filling every space. The sea sucked and
pulled. It was pulling him down the beach.
"I'm coming! I'm coming!" he cried.

A huge wave rolled up the beach. It reared, curled over, and
smashed down upon the sand horse, washing away his mane, his

head, his legs, and his body. It went hissing back down to the sea, dragging the sand horse with it.

The sand horse felt waves buoying him up. Among the waves white horses were prancing. He neighed and tossed his mane.

His hooves struck spray from the sea.
"I can move!" he cried. "I can gallop!"

He frisked and galloped. He swished his white tail.

All around him the white horses plunged and jumped the waves.

"To Sennen!" they neighed. "To Land's End...!"

They galloped away, and the sand horse went with them.

Next morning, when the artist came down to the beach, people
looked at the smooth sand and said, "It's a shame. All that work
washed away."
But the artist smiled.
He knew where his sand horse had gone.